THE WHITE ARCHER

THE WHITE ARCHER

AN ESKIMO LEGEND

WRITTEN AND ILLUSTRATED BY

JAMES HOUSTON

A VOYAGER/HBJ BOOK

HARCOURT BRACE JOVANOVICH

NEW YORK AND LONDON

Copyright © 1967 by James Houston

Printed in the United States of America

67662

LIBRARY OF CONGRESS CATALOGING IN PUBLICATION DATA
Houston, James A   1921–
The white archer.
(A Voyager/HBJ book)
SUMMARY: A young Eskimo vows to avenge his
parents' violent deaths, but over the years that
it takes him to become a master archer, he outgrows
his hatred.
1. Eskimos—Legends. [1. Eskimos—Legends.
2. Indians of North America—Legends] I. Title.
[E99.E7H865   1979]   398.2′1   79-14458
ISBN 0-15-696224-1

First Voyager/HBJ edition 1979

A B C D E F G H I J

In memory of Pootagook and his son Inukjuakjuk
and for the great family that follows them

Kungo raised his head and listened carefully. Somewhere out in the vast Arctic silence of the Ungava, he had heard a strange sound. He remained kneeling on the scrap of white bearskin, listening, but the sound did not come to him again.

He bent down so that his face was level with the man-sized hole in the ice. Motionless, he watched and waited, peering into the shadowy blue depths of the frozen lake. A short time passed, and then a big trout drifted silently beneath him. Its tail waved gently in the current as it moved its fins like small wings to steady itself. Then another trout glided under him, and behind it three more big ones floated like green ghosts in the icy water.

Tightening his grip on a double-pronged fish spear, Kungo took careful aim and drove the shaft downward with a lightning thrust. The bone prongs of the spear slipped over the back of the largest fish, and its curved teeth caught and held. Kungo heaved the struggling fish out of the hole, forced open the prongs of the spear, and released it. The big trout flipped twice on the ice and then lay glazed and still, instantly frozen to death in the intense cold.

Kungo's sister, Shulu, who had been silently fishing with a short hand line at another hole, came quickly across the snow-covered ice. Kungo smiled at her as she picked up the huge fish to feel its weight, for it was half as long as she was.

Kungo's short, strong body was clad in the handsome sealskin parka and pants his mother had made for him. His feet were covered with dark close-fitting sealskin boots that reached his knees. Kungo's hair was very black, his eyes were dark and lively, and when he smiled, his strong teeth flashed brightly against his dark brown skin.

The evening air around them was still and sharp like thinnest crystal that might break at any moment in the bitter cold. The low white hills beside the frozen lake cast long shadows across the snow, and the winter sky blazed like frozen fire as the sun cast its rays at the first pale shadow of the moon.

Using a bone ladle, Shulu filled a sealskin bucket with water from the hole in the ice and followed her brother across the snow-covered surface of the small lake to the hill that lay above their camp. There, Kungo put down the heavy trout, and Shulu rested the bucket on the snow. They looked down at the four snowhouses that were the only dwellings in their tiny village. Around the houses many paths curved through the snow. Two long heavy sleds lay upturned, ready for icing, and three delicate skin-covered kayaks rested high on stone racks away from the sharp teeth of the dogs. The igloos seemed deserted except for the dogs scattered around them, and even they lay quietly as though they were carved in stone. Nothing moved. Everything was silent.

"Our family will be glad to taste that fish," said Shulu. "It's

8

the first to be caught during this moon."

Her tawny brown cheeks glowed like the red throat of an Arctic loon, and her long black hair had a blue sheen like the wings of a raven. She was strong and quick, with endless good humor. Her legs were short, but Kungo knew that she could run like the wind.

As they started down the hill, Kungo stopped suddenly and stared into the cold blue distance. He pointed up the wide river that curved in a long frozen path from the inland plain through the low hills until it reached their camp by the sea.

"Do you see it?" he asked.

She did not answer. Her eyes searched the vast expanse.

"There it is. Moving. Far up the river. It must be a dog team, but who would be coming from the inland to visit us?" Knowing that their own dogs and sleds were in camp, he said, "They must be strangers from far away. Listen. Listen," he repeated, and faintly, like the measured sound of dripping water somewhere out in the vast silence, they heard the "harr, harr, harr. . ." of a driver urging his dogs forward.

Eager to be the first with news that visitors were coming to their lonely camp, Kungo and Shulu hurried down the slope to their father's snowhouse.

When it was almost dark, all the men, women, and children of their small village gathered together before the snowhouses in a silent group, ready to meet the strangers. In the half-light they saw a long heavy sled with three men on it swing into view around the river bend. They watched the strange men cross the wind-swept ice and drive their dogs up the steep bank. Two of the men ran beside the sled, working hard to guide it between the boulders that lay exposed on the icy shore. A third man, bigger than the others, remained half sitting, half lying on the sled.

As the strange team rushed into the camp, wild excitement broke loose, and a dog fight started. Everyone helped to kick and pull apart the two powerful teams until finally the dogs settled down, content for the moment to snarl and stiffly circle each other.

Two of the strangers came forward to greet everyone. Rough men they were, with faces burned dark by the wind and cold, eyebrows white with frost. Their fur clothing was worn and torn, which showed they had not had any women's care or mending for a very long time. Their hair was long and black and wildly tangled. With their hoods pushed back and their mitts left carelessly on the sled, they seemed not to notice the cold. One of the men who had run with the sled, a short, strong man, limped a little as though he had lost some toes long ago from freezing.

Kungo heard his father say to the other driver, a lean man, "I knew you when we were young at the River of Two Tongues. Your father's name was Tunu."

The stranger nodded.

The big man who had remained on the sled raised his left hand in greeting. Kungo looked at his right arm. It hung limp by his side. Kungo could see in the fading light that the sleeve of his tattered parka had a long knife slit in it and that his hand was wet with blood.

Because Kungo's father had known the lean man from the River of Two Tongues, he was bound by politeness to invite the travelers to sleep in his snowhouse. This he did, and the three men gladly accepted. Kungo's mother hurried into the igloo and took her proper place near the edge of the sleeping platform beside the lamp, ready to welcome the strangers to their house. Others in the camp unharnessed and fed the visitors' dogs.

The three men tugged off their worn parkas and lay back on the wide sleeping platform, while the women pulled off their sealskin boots and placed them on the drying rack above the stone lamp filled with seal oil. The big man plucked some soft down from a white bird skin that lay near the lamp and carefully placed it against the long knife wound to stop the bleeding. A seal was cut open for them and prepared for feasting. They greedily drank quantities of fresh cold water and some hot blood soup. After the feast of delicious seal meat, which they had eaten raw, sliced thin, half thawed and half frozen, they lay back in the welcome warmth of the igloo and talked to Kungo's father. The people from the other igloos gathered to hear the news. Everyone listened.

The lean man from the River of Two Tongues recounted their long sled journey. He told of their travels through the range of coastal hills onto the great wind-swept plain in search of caribou. For weeks they had seen nothing but one half-starved wolf. Fierce blizzards had raged inland, and they had gone hungry. Their only food had come from the few ptarmigan they managed to catch. When this news was told, the listeners nodded, for they also knew those small white furry-footed birds inhabiting the inland plain. Their flesh had saved the lives of many travelers. Finally the three men had been forced to eat one of their own dogs, but some time after that they saw a few caribou tracks on the very edge of the Land of Little Sticks.

There they stopped, for it was tree country, dreaded territory belonging to the Indians. The dwarfed trees that grew there were permanently bent by the icy blasts of the north wind. They were few and scattered, and scarcely any of them was taller than a man. There was little soil, and only tundra moss grew there, clinging tightly to the rocks. The Land of Little Sticks was a terrible land, feared by the birds and beasts of the true forest and shunned by the animals that roved the open plain. It was a starving land. Three stone images built to stand like men marked this place. To the south, on the distant horizon, lay vast forest and lake country, a land that suffered a short hot summer alive with black flies and mosquitoes that could drive a man mad.

The Eskimos feared the Indians and their country. The harnesses of their dog teams became entangled in these little stick trees. Ancient Eskimo stories told of terrifying nights spent there, for the wind made the trees moan and whisper like lost souls. Cruel Indians were said to live and hide in this tree country, and no Eskimo considered himself safe there.

Yet the hunger pangs of these three men were so terrible that they overcame all their fear and traveled on and on up the narrow frozen river between the sharp-pointed shadows of the little stick trees. When they climbed a hill to look out over the country for signs of caribou, the big man pointed to a thin wisp of smoke rising in the cold, still air. Frightened they were, but starving as well, and they drew closer until they smelled boiling meat.

The big man, made bold with hunger, left his two hunting companions and the dogs behind and stalked alone through the dreaded trees until he reached a rise in the ground where he could watch the camp. He was careful to stay downwind so that the Indian dogs could not smell him and warn their masters of his presence. He remained there, hiding and watching, from noon until the evening sky turned red. Then he retraced his steps to tell the other two men that the camp was small, having only one tall man, one very old man, a woman, a girl, and two young children. The camp, he said, had only four dogs, which were so small that they looked like starved black foxes. Besides the dogs, they had only one toboggan and a small skin tent hung on poles. But they also had some frozen caribou meat tied up in the trees, safe from their hungry dogs, and rich otter skins stretched on wooden frames for drying.

"I am going to take some of that meat tonight," he said to his companions, "for I am starving."

Pointing to the southeast, his companions replied, "We saw

the smoke of ten fires rising beyond those hills, and we heard the sounds of countless dogs fighting. We warn you, there are many Indians there."

"I care nothing about them," said the big man. "I must have food or else I will die. Will you come with me tonight?"

The two hunters were frightened, but because there was only one sled, there was no way for them to part, and so they finally agreed to go with him. That night when they had carefully anchored the dogs by turning the heavy sled over, they set out for the small Indian camp. In single file they moved cautiously through the dreaded, unfamiliar country. It was deathly cold, and the stars seemed to wheel and dance overhead. The night sky glowed with eerie green northern lights that magically shifted and faded like underwater weeds waving in a river. The trees in the forest cracked loudly with the frost, and dry powder snow, lying on the branches, showered down on the men without warning. All of these things made them nervous, angry, and afraid.

At last they saw the yellow glow of firelight from within the Indian tent, and the big man, again smelling the rich odor of cooking meat, went forward at once. The other two remained at the edge of the clearing. For some time there was silence. Then a dog barked, and then another, and they could hear a man's voice shouting excitedly in a strange language. There was a woman's high-pitched scream and the sound of fighting and more dogs barking. The big man's voice then called to them, shouting their names again and again, and they both ran forward. Their coming must have frightened the Indians, for they

saw no one except the big man, who came stumbling through the soft snow carrying the double haunches of a caribou. They saw his knife glistening in the starlight, and there was blood spattered on his clothing.

They turned and ran hard until they reached their sled, and all that night they drove the dogs along the frozen river until they were safely out of the Land of Little Sticks. In the morning they rested briefly and ate their fill of the stolen caribou meat, giving most of the remainder to their starving dogs. Then they hurried on. They followed the wide flat river course toward the coast and the safety of other Eskimo camps, but they did not return to their own camp at the River of Two Tongues. They knew that the Indians would not venture far from the Land of Little Sticks, for the Indians hated and feared the great treeless, barren land where they could find no wood for their fires nor lodge poles for their tents and became lost traveling in endless circles out on the terrible wind-swept plain.

Kungo's father looked at the three men after he had heard their story and said nothing. In his view they had acted foolishly to be caught starving in the Land of Little Sticks, and certainly they should not have stolen or acted violently. They had broken the laws of the Eskimo people.

The family and the three unwanted guests drifted off into an uneasy sleep only to be awakened twice by the big man who cried out in pain, perhaps because of the knife wound in his arm or because of some terrible dream that had come to haunt him from the Indian camp.

The next day the three men stayed on the sleeping platform

until noon, and although they were not offered food, they made no plans to leave. The big man sat sullen and silent, holding his right arm as he rocked back and forth to ease the pain. His arm and hand had swollen in the night.

The three visitors prepared to spend the second night, and Kungo's father again gave them food. But this time they all ate in silence.

When his father went out of the snowhouse after eating, Kungo followed him, and they stood together in the cold star-filled night. They listened carefully. The father looked up the river from whence the three men had come. He thought of their sled tracks, of their footprints, and even of the drops of blood from the big man's arm that all led straight to the camp. They had left a trail in the snow that even a child could follow. Kungo's father looked at him in a worried way, and Kungo felt the hair stir on the back of his neck, for he knew that the Indian people from the Land of Little Sticks would have good reason to be angry.

Neither Kungo nor his father had ever seen an Indian, although his father had once passed one of their campsites on the edge of the barrens. There he had seen a dead fire and the cleared place where they had pitched their strange tents. Bones and feathers were scattered everywhere, and the smell of smoked skins still lingered in the damp tundra moss.

Kungo followed his father back inside the snowhouse, where the three men were already asleep. Kungo's mother smiled at her husband and son as she trimmed the wick in her seal-oil lamp until it caused a gentle glow to reflect from the glistening snow walls. She then arranged the boots on the rack over the lamp so they would be dry in the morning.

On this night Kungo slept in his clothes with his head toward the foot of the sleeping platform, which is sometimes the custom of young boys when the only bed of the house is crowded with guests. He slowly drifted off to sleep and dreamed of peering through the hole in the lake ice, where he saw a hidden world wrapped in green shadows with fishlike people swimming among strange houses that looked like igloos piled one upon the other.

Suddenly he awoke. What he saw was not a dream. Strange men with dark hats were crowding into the low entrance of the snowhouse, filling the room with their harsh words and violent movements. He saw a knife flash. Then someone kicked over the lamp. In the dark there was angry shouting, screaming, and the sound of stabbing. Kungo jumped up as he felt a sharp cut on his ankle. Clinging to the wall, he crouched down and felt his way around the edge of the house until he came to the entrance. Bending low, he rushed past a tall, gaunt man who smelled of smoke. The man tried to grab him as he ran out into the night, but he was able to break away. Where could he go? The house was full of fear, of shouting, of words and sounds he had never heard before.

Kungo ran past the neighboring igloo and beyond the rack of kayaks until he reached the snowhouse of his uncle and aunt. They were both sitting up in bed, terrified by the sounds they heard. They quickly grabbed him and hid him under the thick pile of caribou skins on the bed, and then they lay on top of him. He heard running footsteps and more strange voices. A man rushed in looking for him, but seeing only two old people in bed, the Indian grunted with disgust and hurried out again.

When the first light of day allowed them to see, Kungo poked a small hole in the wall of his uncle's snowhouse and looked toward his father's igloo. One wall had been broken in, and their household things were scattered everywhere. He saw no movement.

In front of the house he counted eleven Indians. Tall, thin men they were, with faces made terrible by painted black streaks. They were wearing strange pointed hats and long coats with weird markings. Each man carried a bow or club or knife in his hand. They were calling to each other in excited voices. Several of them were shooting arrows into the igloo and into the bearskin and two sealskins that were stretched out to dry. With their knives they had slashed the pelts and cut the sealskin dog lines into pieces. They had pulled the kayaks from their racks, had ripped them open, and had smashed their long, delicate frames. They were gathering all the food they could find, and they were preparing to go.

Suddenly Kungo caught a glimpse of his sister, Shulu. He watched with terror as the Indians led her down toward one of their toboggans on the river.

Then as dawn turned the village gray, they started to search the other igloos again. Kungo's aunt quickly made him put on her long-tailed woman's parka and handed him a skin bucket. Disguised as an old woman, he bent over, his head hidden deep in the hood, and hobbled away from the igloo. He went off toward the side of the village as though he were going to the

lake to get water. Halfway through the camp he saw one of the strangers, the big man, lying face down on the snow with two arrows in his back, his bloody arm flung out stiffly before him.

Out of the corner of his eye, Kungo saw an Indian point at him and another place an arrow in his bow and take aim. The arrow whistled past his face and buried itself in the snow. Fortunately the Indian did not aim again. Kungo hobbled over the hill beyond their sight. Once at the lake, he threw off his aunt's parka and snatched up a broken ivory-bladed snow knife that lay by a hole in the ice. Then he ran.

He ran as far and as fast as he could. He headed northward, following the coastline so he would not lose his way. Far up beyond the River of Giant Men, he knew there were Eskimo people who would help him.

When night came, he struggled to find strength to go on. He lay in the snow, exhausted, and his eyes filled with tears as he thought of the fate of his mother and father, his relatives, and his sister, Shulu. Then slowly a terrible anger started to grow within him. Dark thoughts rushed through his mind. He had only twelve winters of life upon him, but if he could live to reach the next Eskimo camp, he swore inside himself that he would avenge the terrible wrong done his family by the people from the Land of Little Sticks. He pounded the hard snow with his fists and swore this to himself, again and again.

He was afraid to build a snowhouse for fear he might be followed, and when he had rested a little, he went on despite the darkness, because he knew that if he slept without shelter, he would freeze to death. To avoid leaving a trail, he traveled along wind-packed drifts that were so hard his footsteps left no mark.

Worn out and starving and driven by fear, he slowly made his way north. After the first night he would cut blocks out of the frozen snow and pile them in a circle to form a house scarcely big enough for a dog. Some nights it was so cold that he could not sleep, but the little houses protected him against the biting wind that swept in from the frozen sea, and he was able to stay alive. He lost count of the number of snowhouses he built and the days he limped through the killing cold. The knife slash in his ankle pained him.

One evening, a seal hunter called Inukpuk, returning to his camp after hunting out on the sea ice, saw the boy staggering half frozen among the ice hummocks near the shore. He carried Kungo to his sled, wrapped him in a caribou skin, and put his arm around his shoulders to steady him. Inukpuk got the boy safely back to camp, where his wife put him into the center of their warm bed and fed him hot blood soup and little pieces of rich seal meat. She cared for him like a mother until he was well and strong again.

For two long years he stayed with Inukpuk and his wife, watching and waiting as each season advanced across the land. He searched for eggs and fished with the other young people of the camp, but there was a dark and fearful quietness that seemed to brood inside him. He never spoke of the fate of his parents, or of his sister, or of the people of the Little Sticks, but they were always in his mind.

In the late autumn of the second year, after the first big snow had turned everything white so that the dog teams could travel again, a hunter came with his son from a camp farther to the north. One evening he told a long story of a visit he had made to a distant island that could only be reached by sled during the two moons of midwinter. There he had met a strange old man full of mystery, with a knowledge of the ways of men and animals. His eyes and body seemed weak, but he could draw a huge horn bow that the strongest man among them could not even bend, and his old eyes could still see well enough to drive an arrow straight to its mark no matter how far or how small. His wife, it was said, could hand-stitch the seams of a kayak with sinew so that no water could ever enter, and she could so tightly sew a cut in a man's skin that one could never see the stitches. Their only sadness, said the hunter, was that they had no children. The old man had said that he would soon go blind.

During the night, Kungo thought about all that he had heard, and in the morning he said to Inukpuk and his wife, "I give thanks to you for your kindness, for you have saved my life and been a family to me. But now I wish to travel north with that man who visits and his son, if they will take me, for I long to see that old man on the island and talk with him."

Inukpuk said that he would be glad if Kungo would stay in their camp and be a son to them. But Kungo only thanked them again and said once more that he wished to go north.

The visiting seal hunter agreed to take Kungo to his camp, and so they set out one dark and windy morning in early winter when the snow was hard and the sled could move fast. Inukpuk's wife had made Kungo new sealskin boots and mitts. She gave them to him for the journey, and Inukpuk gave him two seals, one to help feed the dogs on the trip north and one as a gift for the people in the new camp.

After saying farewell, they traveled north for five days, following the coast through a frozen empty land. During their journey they crossed only one fox track and saw no other sign of life save two thin ravens that croaked loudly as they chased and tumbled with each other across the evening sky.

On the fifth night Kungo saw the glow of lights from the ice windows of the three snowhouses in the seal hunter's camp, and the dogs raced forward, delighted to be home at last. Everyone came out to welcome the returning travelers, and they showed Kungo every sign of friendship.

The long, hard snowdrifts were driven high against the hills, and Kungo waited patiently for the midwinter moons when the weather would be even colder and the sea hard frozen, and when the sun would not light the river valleys.

The seal hunter knew that to go to the island was very important to Kungo, and for this reason he planned to make the trip. His wife was worried, for she knew the danger of crossing by sled from the mainland to the island because the great tides could at any moment tear out the ice bridge between the two. When they were preparing to make the perilous journey, she begged her husband not to take their son, for she feared that they might both be lost to her, and to this he agreed.

Kungo helped the hunter ice the lightest and fastest sled in the camp, spitting a mouthful of water along the upturned runners and polishing it into icy smoothness with a scrap of bearskin. The other hunters lent the seal hunter their strongest dogs so that the sled would go swiftly, and they loaded it with nothing save two thick fur sleeping skins, a harpoon, a snow knife, and a seal for food.

They traveled north along the coast and slept three nights on the way. Then they turned outward on the frozen sea, and Kungo realized the terrible hazards that lay before them. The barren rock island was hidden from view, wrapped in whirling drifts of snow. Dark patches of open water and frightening black holes showed dangerously against the whiteness of the snow-covered ice. In the bitter cold these open holes threw up gray fog against the darkened sky, and mists froze and fell back like snow into the black water. Many times the hunter had to walk before the dogs, feeling with his harpoon for a safe passage across the treacherous sea ice that was broken by the rising and falling tides.

At last Kungo saw stretching out toward the island a great ice bridge, and they started along this narrow strip. But soon it grew dark and the wind rose, and they were forced to stop for the night. There was no snow there to build an igloo, just naked ice, and the howling wind swept down from the north with increasing fury. The hunter and Kungo turned their sled on its side to give them protection against the wind and rolled themselves up in the sleeping skins. With the dogs huddled around them, they managed to stay alive. Kungo lay shivering, listening in fear and wonder to the great sighing of the new-formed ice. If the ice bridge broke, they would drown in the freezing waters.

As if by magic, in the early morning the wind died, and the hunter sat up and looked around him. The air was still now, and the whirling snow had faded away.

26

There, plainly visible, lay the island, known as Tugjak. It was high and rocky, the point of a hidden mountain thrusting its stone head out of the frozen sea. Only in one place were the sheer rock walls broken by a narrow cleft. Around the island was a huge ice ledge, and beyond this was a rough broken collar of ice chunks that rose and fell with the moving tides. Snow filled every crack in the dark rocks, but the hard, smooth places were all blown clear by the savage winds that roared over the island.

The hunter drove his team along the ice ledge on the south face of the island cliffs toward the narrow opening in the rock wall. The entrance to the steep passage stood before them like a needle's eye. They began the climb, and so hard was the ascent that they often had to help the dogs to find footing. At length they reached a narrow slit in the top of the cliff. It led into a huge round place surrounded by rust-colored granite walls rising higher than a man could throw a stone. It was roofless—and so wide that Kungo thought he could not cross it in a hundred leaps.

At the base of this stone room, there were many entrances into dark caves and passages, and higher up among the steep, smooth rocks, there were narrow walks and holes in the stone wall that looked like windows.

Kungo followed the hunter forward across the open, snow-carpeted area until they came to a small house half buried in the ground, with walls that were shoulder high and made of stone. The roof beams of the house were the ribs of whales, covered with large sealskins weighted in place with a thick layer of sod. On either side of the entrance stood the great jawbones of a whale.

As they peered at this strange entrance, wondering what to do, a dwarf man pushed aside the sealskin curtain that served as a door for the house and waved them inside. He had powerful arms and shoulders and a twisted back, and his hair was long and knotted in the ancient style. He smiled at them in a shy and kindly way when they entered.

It was dark inside the little stone house, and Kungo crouched in the entrance passage, waiting for his eyes to become accustomed to the light. He saw the old woman first as she sat tending her stone lamp that was shaped like a half-moon. It burned with an even white flame, reflecting across the pool of rich seal fat that was its fuel. The old woman nodded and smiled and beckoned at them to come and sit beside her on the sleeping platform.

Kungo observed her carefully. Her warm brown face was flat and wide, with powerful jaw muscles that drew the flesh tight over her high cheekbones. Her eyes were jet black, and as she looked at Kungo again, they shone warmly, revealing all the hidden power of life within her. Her eyelids had been drawn narrow by a whole lifetime in the wind and snow and sun. Around her eyes and mouth and spreading up across her forehead, there appeared countless tiny wrinkles like the fine grain in an ancient piece of driftwood. When she smiled, her strong white teeth clamped together, worn evenly from chewing and softening numberless sealskins. Her hair, black and much thinner now than when she had been a girl, was caught in two tight braids that coiled neatly around her ears. Not one gray hair showed.

Bending forward, the old woman made a seat for Kungo, and he noticed that her short body, like her eyes, gave him the feeling of someone with quickness and hidden strength. Her round brown wrists had delicate blue tattooing on them, which had been done for her when she was a child. Her hands were strong and square. The right thumb and forefinger were bent and powerful from forcing bone needles through thick animal skins.

Kungo was startled when he sat down. He had not noticed beside her the old man kneeling on the sleeping platform. This ancient Eskimo was as motionless as though he were carved of stone. The light from the lamp did not seem to touch him, and he remained wrapped in shadows.

"My husband has been away in the storm," said the old woman. "Now he is back and resting. He will wake soon. You two have had a long trip and must be hungry."

She waved to the dwarf, who placed horn bowls of melted ice water, a dark red saddle of young walrus meat, and sun-dried strips of trout before them, and the hunter and Kungo ate quickly. Then the old woman cleverly drew the flame along the lamp's wick until it made the whole house glow with a soft, even light.

When Kungo was filled, he wiped his hands and mouth with a soft bird skin. He stole another glance at the old man, who remained motionless in the same position. But now the ancient wrinkled face and hands seemed to glow like ivory, and there was light around the old man's long white hair and the thin traces of his beard. His eyelids fluttered and opened, he slowly turned his head, and he looked at Kungo with eyes that were dark green and shadowy like pools of water on the sea ice.

"You have arrived," he said in a deep voice that made Kungo know he must be a great singer.

"Yes, we have arrived," answered Kungo in the most formal manner, for he felt both fear and respect for this old man.

"You have had a long journey, and now it is time for you both to sleep," said the old man. "I shall think a while and decide what will be best for you now that you are here. Sleep," he said again, "sleep."

The seal hunter and Kungo lay back on the soft caribou furs, glad to be safe in the warmth of this old stone house. Kungo looked up and wondered at the mighty ribs that curved across the low ceiling, and as he drifted off to sleep, he imagined himself inside the living body of a whale as it plunged into the depths of the sea.

When he awoke the next morning, light streamed down through the thin, transparent window above the door. The window was made of stretched seal intestine carefully sewn together by the old woman and was the only source of daylight in the house. Kungo sat up quickly when he realized that the seal hunter had already gone.

"He left very early," said the old woman, nodding above her

lamp. "He wished to cross the ice bridge while the weather remained fair and the wind gentle. He asked me to say farewell to you. My husband, Ittok, has gone out, too, for he has always loved to watch the dawning of each new day."

Kungo bent low at the small entrance, and once outside, he breathed deeply in the clear, sharp air. No one was in sight. He looked up at the pale light of day brightening the eastern sky, and then he noticed a movement in one of the entrances in the rock wall. The old man walked slowly out into the daylight. He leaned heavily on the powerful dwarf, one arm draped across the little man's hunched shoulders. As they made their way toward him, Kungo noticed in the old man's free hand a great thick bow.

"You have come to learn, and I am here to teach," said the old man, in his deep rich voice. "This," he added, holding up the bow, "this is Kigavik, the dark falcon, swiftest hunter of them all."

He placed one end of the bow against the frozen ground, and with a swift, powerful downward motion, he bent it and slipped the bowstring over the end notch. This bow was of a size and strength that Kungo had never known. It was made of musk-ox horn from the Eskimo place they call the Land Behind the Sun. It was polished smooth and bound in many places with the finest braided caribou sinew. Best of all, it was beautifully shaped, swept back like the outstretched wings of a plunging falcon. Never had there been such a bow.

Ittok offered it to Kungo, who held it in his hands like a precious treasure. He placed his hand on the string, and the touch made it sing like the east wind.

"Now, draw the bow," said the old man.

Kungo drew back hard, but the braided sinew did not move.

"Draw the bow," said Ittok once again.

It would not move.

"Draw the bow," Ittok commanded.

Taking a deep breath and using all his strength, Kungo managed to draw it back until it reached its full curve.

"Look! See that! See!" the old man called out in excitement to the dwarf. "You who can crack stones with your teeth and break the back of a white bear with your strong arms cannot draw that bow. But this boy, he can draw the bow. He can make the falcon sing. Look. He will be an archer. Perhaps he will be a great archer. Tomorrow our long task will begin."

Together, Kungo and the dwarf helped Ittok back into the house, where they carefully unstrung Kigavik and wrapped it safely in soft skins. Kungo's hands trembled as he looked at the great bow and thought of the fate of his family. "Revenge! Revenge! With a bow such as this I could have revenge!" The thought cut through him like a cruel wind.

That evening they picked rich marrow from the soft centers of caribou bones and ate the sweet flesh of young sea birds that had been preserved in seal oil. When the feast was over, the old man lay back among the thick caribou skins and went to sleep, and the dwarf left the small house for the freezing caves where he slept.

Kungo watched the old woman sew a new pair of sealskin boots. Her stitches were so small that he could not see them. She asked him about his mother, and slowly he told her the story of his life, which until now he had told no one. He spoke of his love for his parents and his sister, Shulu, and of that terrible night when the Indians had come, the night when his whole life had changed. Though he had never before revealed his innermost feelings, he told the old woman every hidden thought within him, every hate and joy, fear and longing. To Kungo she did not seem like other people. She was somehow like the earth itself. Speaking with her, he had the same feeling he had when he lay on soft tundra, warmed by the summer sun, and looked up at the wide blue sky. Then he felt he could understand every word of the wind's song. She was that kind of person.

When he had told her everything, he felt a great relief and went to sleep immediately. The old woman rose stiffly from her place on the sleeping platform and gently spread a warm caribou skin over her old husband and the young sleeping boy. Then she returned to her sewing.

During the late winter moon, the dwarf, whose name Telikjuak means big arms, told Kungo many things about their island home. He showed him the way through the numerous passages inside the granite cliffs that surrounded the little house, and the place where he, Telikjuak, slept. It was a small stone room, icy cold, with nothing in it save the skin of a huge white bear that lay neatly folded on a rock ledge that served as his bed. He showed Kungo the two rear entrances to the caves. One led to the small deep lake where they got fresh water, the other opened at the place where the dogs were kept. Beyond the high rock, the island of Tugjak stretched north, and there they often walked along the cliffs, scanning the frozen sea, looking for walrus or whales in the big open pools of water.

From the time of his arrival, Kungo helped Telikjuak to feed and care for the ten strong sled dogs. The dwarf taught him how to rule the big dogs without fear and to respect the white female lead dog named Lao. It was she who led the strong team and responded quickly to the driver's orders. She was not the strongest fighter, but she was always protected by the biggest male dog in the team. Lao soon began to rub her thick white coat against Kungo's leg and to lick his hands when he came to feed her.

One winter night when the air was still and cold and the moon rose up bone-white and calm as a sleeper's face, Kungo heard the long, lonely howl of a white wolf far away on the other end of the island, where rocky crags plunged straight down to the frozen sea. The eerie sound came to him again and again, and he heard Lao answer the white wolf with a high moaning that he had never known before.

Kungo hurried to the sheltered place where the dog team slept, but Lao was already gone. She was running fast across the hard-packed snow toward the far end of the island. When he turned to enter the passage again, he found Telikjuak standing beside him.

"That big white wolf will kill your little Lao," said Telikjuak.

But he was wrong.

The next day Kungo found Lao back with the team. She seemed tired from her long run but contented. Later, in the spring, Lao grew big, and Kungo built a small snowhouse for her.

One morning he heard her snarling viciously at the other dogs, and looking into her small house, he found that she had eight newborn pups. All of them were white as snow. She let Kungo pick one up to examine it. It had a longer muzzle and larger ears than a husky. Its legs were long and thin, and its feet splayed wide, which would be good for running swiftly on the snow. This was no ordinary pup that Kungo held. It was half wolf and half dog.

Kungo hurried back to the house to tell the news to Ittok and the old woman.

Laughing with delight, the old man said, "If you can raise those children of the white wolf, they will be yours. Wolves are not as strong as dogs, but they are fast and tireless and need little food."

Soon after, the dwarf appeared and spread a large scraped sealskin on the edge of the sleeping platform. On this he placed some long caribou rib bones and a pile of strong sinews that had been drawn from a caribou's back. Beside these he laid several short knives, a sharpening stone, and two special pieces of bone, one for straightening arrows and the other for bending the bow.

Then the old man and the boy began their long task. Slowly they shaped and matched the strong springy rib bones and cut them so they fitted together perfectly into one piece to make a delicate curving bow.

While they worked, the old woman sat silently by her lamp, and with skilled hands she spread the sinews apart with a little horn comb. Then she spun and knotted them between her nimble fingers until they became long strands of strong brown thread.

These she braided together into thin cords. They were each as fine as a single blade of grass, and yet they could easily carry the whole weight of a man. She dampened these cords with snow water and handed them to the old man, who slowly bound each piece of bone in place with the sinew cords. He then ran the cords up and down along the whole length of the bow many times until the strands lay evenly together. These strands he bound tightly to the bow. When the cords dried, they gripped the bow like a falcon's claw and gave springing power to it.

Now the old woman handed them the strongest double-braided strand of all, the bowstring itself, made from the center sinew of a bull caribou's back. When the bone bow was flexed and the bowstring gripped the notch, it drew all the long sinews tight and gave added strength. The bow was much smaller than the great Kigavik and felt lighter in Kungo's hand. It was white like a young falcon. It was made for him, and he wished more than anything to become skilled with it quickly.

A few days later when the bow was finished, they began to make the arrows. The old man took long pieces of caribou bone, split them, shaped them, and bound them together. At the end of each shaft he made a slit, and into this he forced a slim stone arrowhead made of hardest slate. The old man had shown Kungo how to shape and sharpen each head. At the other end of each arrow, after it was notched, they bound the dark wing feathers of a raven to the shaft to guide the arrow in its flight.

When their work was finished, the old woman handed Kungo a trim quiver made of sealskin with two compartments, one for the new bow and the other for the arrows.

40

The long white Arctic spring faded as the sun of summer wheeled above the island. Everywhere the soft gray tundra moss appeared through the snow, and the tiny Arctic flowers unfolded like colored stars. Small birds returned from warm lands in the south and sang their songs as they hopped about gathering dried moss for their nests. The weather softened, and warm mists rose in the early mornings. It was a joy to hear the faint bird sounds after the long silence of winter, for it was as though the whole world were being born again. The sun never left the sky.

"Set up a target, boy," said the old man early one morning. "It is time you learned to use the new bow."

In great excitement Kungo ran out and hurriedly built up two targets with the last soft snow that remained against the north wall hidden from the sun. One target was a model of a bear, the other the likeness of a man.

When Kungo returned to the little house, the old man and the dwarf were waiting for him.

"Are you an enemy of all white bears?" asked the old man.

Kungo thought about this question for a moment.

"No," he answered, "but I hope that one day a white bear will offer himself to me."

"Then do not drive arrows into his image or all white bears will be offended. And men, Kungo, would you do harm to all men?"

"No," said Kungo quickly. "I seek eleven bowmen. Those will I harm. Those I will kill."

"Hear me well, Kungo," Ittok said. "Do not give men cause to fear you, for one who does that is no better than a dog gone mad, wishing only to bite and kill."

Ittok waved his hand, and the dwarf hobbled across and cut out two large square blocks of snow, placed one upon the other, and in the center of the upper block stuck a dark piece of tundra moss about the size of a man's hand.

The old man stepped forward. He took Kungo's new bow and stood for a moment as though he were in deep thought. Then scarcely looking at the target, he aimed, drew back the bowstring, and released it. Although he had not placed an arrow in the bow, he said to Telikjuak that he was out of practice and had missed the mark.

Again the old man seemed lost in thought, and again he drew the bow without an arrow. He released the bowstring and said that this time he had struck the mark.

"Now, Kungo, it is your turn."

Kungo raised the bow, aimed, quickly drew back the empty bowstring, and released it.

The old man stepped forward beside him and said, "You must learn to shoot the bow and guide the arrows with your mind, for it is only with the power of your thoughts that you will become a great archer. Imagine that you have a true arrow. Draw and release it, and guide it quickly with your eye and mind straight to the mark."

Kungo concentrated, drawing the bow again and again without using an arrow.

"Now practice each day," commanded Ittok. "Practice until your mind is tired and your fingers bleed on the bowstring, and at the end of summer I shall let you use one of your arrows."

42

Kungo's mind flashed backward to the dreaded scene that haunted him, waking or sleeping—the scene of his father's broken snowhouse and his sister being taken away. He gripped his throat to keep from screaming out in anger. He must do as the old one commanded.

During the short summer Kungo practiced long and hard. Sometimes he saw the old man and the dwarf watching him from the entrance of the dark caves, but they said not a word.

One morning when he awoke there was a light fall of snow on the ground, almost covering the autumn red of the tundra, and the little ponds were covered with a thin sheet of ice.

When he went outside with his bow, the old man and Telikjuak were waiting for him. Ittok handed him a single arrow. Black feathered it was and long, with a sharp tip. Kungo felt a surge of wild excitement as he placed the arrow in his bow. He aimed at the small target of woven hide and released the arrow. It flew wide of the mark and struck harmlessly in the tundra.

"Bring it back quickly," cried the old man, and Kungo ran across the wide space and returned with the arrow.

"Now, think," said Ittok. "Think what you are trying to do. Guide the arrow with your eye. Force it with your mind to go straight to the mark."

Kungo drew the bow again and held it until it seemed to him that the feathered shaft reached in and touched the very center of his being. Then he released the arrow, and it flew straight down the course, following his line of vision until it struck the center of the target.

"Good!" shouted the old man, and Telikjuak smiled and

nodded his head at Kungo. "You have it now. Practice with that black arrow until the midwinter moon and I, an old man, shall take you hunting."

After they had gone, Kungo stood alone surrounded by the great stone walls and thought again, fiercely, of why he wanted to be a great bowman. Only he could avenge the wrong done to his family. Concentrating once more, he raised the bow and with an easy rhythm drove the arrow straight through the heavy target.

Slowly winter came to them, and it was dark until noon each day. Savage winds blew in from the frozen sea and seemed to hold the land in an icy grasp. A new bridge of ice formed solidly between the mainland and their island home. The old woman had completed her work on their winter clothes, and Telikjuak had prepared the long sled and harnesses for the big dogs. They were ready for the journey.

They planned to leave Lao on the island to fend for her growing family of young white wolf dogs, knowing she would teach them to dig beneath the snow for lemming and to catch hare and ptarmigan to feed themselves.

On a clear day Telikjuak loaded the sled down on the sea ice. Kungo and the old woman helped Ittok down the high snowy passage from their home. Once they were on the sled, Kungo was surprised at Ittok's agility. He sat beside his wife, and although his eyes and legs were weak, his arms were strong, and he rode the sled cleverly, balancing and shifting his weight as they crossed the rough ice. Ittok called commands to the new lead dog in his deep songlike voice, and the dog obeyed instantly.

45

Kungo and the powerful dwarf sat on the long sled or ran beside it, guiding it across the snow.

That night they slept near the end of the ice bridge, close to the land, where snow had drifted. The dwarf and Kungo built a new igloo, and when it was completed, the old woman hurried inside to spread the sleeping skins neatly over the snow bench. She took a live spark from a small stone tinder box that she carried when traveling, blew it into a flame, and lighted the wick in her little seal-oil lamp.

When the dogs were fed and the men entered the igloo, they placed the thick snow door neatly over the entrance and ate some tasty strips of seal meat. The old woman pulled off their boots and placed them carefully on the drying rack over the lamp. She looked around her new house and saw the white walls glistening like diamonds. She laughed out loud with pleasure, for she loved to travel.

The next day they journeyed beyond the ice of the sea and moved inland, following a flat river course through the coastal hills. The wind blew violently, and that night they built a strong igloo in the protection of the riverbank. Snow whipped into the air until they could not see each other or the dogs, and they were forced to remain in this snowhouse for three days until the storm died.

When they went out once more into the fresh white world, their dogs were buried deeply in the snow, sleeping comfortably in the warmth of their heavy fur coats with their tails curled above their noses so they could breathe.

Now they traveled for five long days across the white flatness

46

of the inland plain, where land and sky were joined together in a long unbroken line. Sometimes on a wind-swept place the old man told Kungo to set up one stone upon another to mark their trail so that they could trace their way back out of the flat land in case they ever came this way again. On the fourth day they crossed a few caribou tracks, and on the fifth day there were a great many fresh tracks.

They stopped early in the afternoon and built a snowhouse larger than the others of the trip, and on its front they built a small meat porch. This igloo had a clear ice window over the door and a long tunnel entrance to keep out the wind, as they expected to stay here for some time.

The old woman started fixing the inside of the new house, beating the snow out of the sleeping skins to make them dry and comfortable. Kungo heard her singing to herself an ancient song as she lighted the flame of her lamp:

> "Ayii, Ayii,
> Even as a spirit
> Joyfully I'll roam
> Down every river valley
> That leads toward the sea.
> Ayii, Ayii."

That night as they lay among the furs on the sleeping bench, they began to talk. This was the time Kungo liked best, for it was a time to speak, to listen, and to learn. The old man said to Kungo, "Being a hunter is many things. To be a clever bowman is not enough. First you must know where to find the animals, and then when you have found them, you must know how to stalk them on this flat plain or out on the open ice of the sea. A man does not just kill because he is a clever hunter. He succeeds in the hunt only if he is a good man, a wise man, who obeys the rules of life. If the animals or birds or fish see that a man is cruel and stupid, they will not give themselves to him.

"Tomorrow, if the weather is good," continued Ittok, "you will hunt with Telikjuak. He is slow with his legs, but he has become wise with his mind. Do not take a bow or spear with you. Telikjuak does not need such weapons, for he was born among the caribou people and he knows many ways to stalk the animals on the plain."

In the morning, the dwarf and Kungo dressed in their warmest caribou skin clothing, for a light wind was blowing out of the west and it was bitter cold. Kungo shyly handed a pair of wooden snow goggles to Telikjuak, for he had carved two pairs of narrow-slitted goggles during the long blizzard. Telikjuak thanked him and said that now they would not go blind in the glaring whiteness. Telikjuak rolled two skins tightly and tied them across his back, and he showed Kungo how to place a long knife inside his skin boot.

After walking some distance, they came to a slight rise in the ground. The dwarf quickly led Kungo up it, hobbling very fast with his short broken way of hop-walking. When they were on the highest ground, the dwarf showed Kungo how to hold his mittened hands together. Telikjuak then hopped up lightly into Kungo's hands and stepped onto his shoulders. From this height he searched the country with his hawklike eyes and then quickly hopped down.

Kungo looked around carefully and said, "I see nothing."

"Come with me," said Telikjuak. "Just beyond the river there are as many caribou as I have fingers and toes. They are difficult to see when they are lying down, for their backs are almost white with frost from their breathing."

The dwarf then led Kungo on a long walk across the plain.

"Are we near them now?" whispered Kungo while searching hard with his eyes.

"No. We are farther from them," said Telikjuak. "But we are downwind of them, and they will not smell us here. Sit down and rest."

Telikjuak quickly spread one caribou skin over his shoulders and sat down on the lowest part. Kungo did the same with the other skin.

"Look," the dwarf whispered. "They're up and moving, feeding at that place where the wind has blown the tundra clear of snow."

For the first time, Kungo saw the caribou, twenty of them, pale as silver ghosts, blending with the snow and sky.

Telikjuak rose slowly, and bending over, he blew his breath across the dark hairs of the skin so that frost formed and made the skin silvery and difficult to see. It looked exactly like the caribou before them. Then he drew the soft hide around his shoulders until the front legs hung over his arms and the back legs hung down by his feet. The head poked out stiffly in front of him, the big ears spread wide.

"Like this," he said, and started off, bent over and moving slowly upwind like a feeding caribou.

Kungo mimicked the movements of the dwarf and was soon astonished to find himself within a dog team's length of the nearest animal. Then the dwarf slowly led Kungo into the very center of the herd, and none of the animals seemed to notice them.

Kungo saw that caribou were all around. They were so close that he could almost touch them. A bull caribou with a huge rack of antlers suddenly raised his head and snorted loudly, having smelled something. Kungo stiffened in his tracks. But the dwarf moved on, imitating a feeding caribou, and the big bull soon settled down to feed again right beside Kungo. The dwarf under the hide glanced slyly at Kungo and smiled. Kungo knew that he must decide what to do next.

Slowly, very slowly, he reached down and drew the long knife from its sheath in his boot top, and with a short, powerful movement, he drove it into the bull caribou's chest. The animal gave a great leap that tore the knife from Kungo's hand, stumbled a few paces, and then with a sigh sank to its knees. The spirit rushed out of it, and it was dead. The other caribou looked at it for a moment, but believing that it was resting, they continued to graze.

The dwarf walked on among the animals, imitating their

movements perfectly. He seemed not to notice that Kungo had killed a caribou. Kungo watched him carefully, wondering what Telikjuak would do next, wondering also what he himself should do.

Suddenly the dwarf threw off his caribou-skin cover and stood upright, a man among the animals. Their antlers flashed upwards as they saw him for the first time. They snorted with alarm and bounded away, scattering in different directions. Their great splayed hoofs carried them swiftly across the snow, but soon they banded together, once more drawn by their instincts as a herd. In a few moments they were almost out of sight, leaving behind them a whirling cloud of snow crystals. All, that is, save Kungo's dead caribou and two others who stood motionless.

"Start walking behind that one," called the dwarf to Kungo. "Move toward our camp. Keep it before you. We can come back for your dead caribou tomorrow with the dogs and sled to haul it in."

The two caribou moved slowly in front of them as though dazed, and Kungo realized that the dwarf had stabbed them both so quickly that he had not seen the motion. Telikjuak had stabbed them lightly in a special place behind the chest so that they could still walk. In this way the two hunters easily guided the caribou back to the snowhouse. One fell within a dog team's length of the igloo; the other dropped over right at the entrance.

"That is how to stalk and kill an animal," cried the old man, who stood beside the snowhouse watching them drive the caribou home. He held himself stiffly upright, supported by the big bow, and his old eyes glowed with pride as he thought of the boy becoming a man. With excitement he called to the old woman, asking her to come and help them with the skinning. He warned the dogs away from the caribou with a harsh command.

The next day Kungo went out with the sled to bring in his caribou, but a starving wolf had found it in the night, and he brought back less than half the meat.

Slowly as the days passed, the air became warmer, and in the early mornings they heard the short, shrill mating call of the white-feathered ptarmigan. Bare patches of tundra started to show through the snow. The old man was slowly carving a piece of antler into the likeness of a caribou. This carving he rubbed and polished carefully, for he believed that such a friendly act would cause the caribou to wish to give themselves to the hunters.

Because the spirit of the hunt was still strong in him, the old man sometimes took Kigavik and, using it like a staff, wandered slowly up the river hoping to find game. One evening, Kungo met Ittok, and they rested together before making their way back to the camp. The old man told Kungo of a great journey northward to the Land Behind the Sun he had taken when he had been young and strong and his eyes could see great distances. Throwing back his head, Ittok drew in a deep breath and in a rich voice sang a song about the musk ox and about the joy he had had in that far-off place:

"Ayii, Ayii, Ayii, Ayii,
  Wondering I saw them,
  Great black beasts,
  Running, standing,
  Eating flowers on the high plain.
  On my belly I crept to them
  With my bow and arrows in my mouth.
  The big one reared up in surprise
  As my arrow quivered in his chest.
  The herd scattered
  Running on the high plain,
  And small I sat singing
  By the big bull's side.
  Ayii, Ayii."

The old woman was always busy and full of singing as she mended their clothes, dried their boots, and scraped the new skins.

One day she told Kungo that she had placed some round black stones on the ice of a lake half a day's journey from their camp. Now she wanted to go and see if the sun had heated them enough to drop them through the thick lake ice and make holes for fishing.

Together they walked out across the land, and with every step they responded to the wonder of the quick Arctic spring as it burst around them. They could hear the water running in streams beneath the snow. So well did Kungo and the old woman understand each other that they did not often feel the need to speak.

Reaching the lake, they both stopped, sensing something strange. Then Kungo saw it. It was a pure black kasigiak, a rare freshwater seal, lying out on the ice near the opposite shore.

"A beautiful skin," said the old woman softly. "That skin could make the best pair of boots in the land. Hurry, boy, before it sees you and dives down into its hole in the ice. Kasigiaks are very easily disturbed."

Scarcely moving, Kungo drew his bow from its case and carefully fitted an arrow to the bowstring. He paused, looking at the ground, thinking only of the black seal. Then with a smooth, even swing, he raised the bow and sent the deadly arrow winging along its course, straight into the animal's heart. The seal scarcely moved as its soul rushed out of its body.

"It was a long way to that seal. I see now that you will become a great archer," said the old woman with joy in her voice as they started out across the ice. Swiftly and cleverly she removed the richly spotted skin from the seal with her sharp moon-faced woman's knife. Cutting away the thick layer of white fat, she exposed the dark red meat underneath.

"When I was very young," she said, "and it was spring, I once came walking here with my grandmother to fish. Six days we stayed, yet she carried no food, no tent, no snow knife, only a little bone hook and fishing line hidden in her hood. When evening came, we lay down near a stone for protection and slept out under the open sky. My grandmother was a strong woman, full of ancient songs. She would put me on her back when I was a child and walk all day to catch one fish. Come now, we must eat meat, for meat in a man is like oil in a lamp. It gives one strength and heat from within."

After they had eaten their fill, Kungo lay down on a high piece of dry tundra with the snow around him and watched the stars come out and grow bright as the sky darkened, and he thought again, as he often did, that there would be no real peace or joy for him till he had avenged the death of his parents.

The next morning he awoke and saw the sun was high, shedding its warmth over the land. There were bird sounds all around him. The old woman was already down at the new fishing holes made in the ice by the stones. She was fishing diligently with her small hook and hand line. Three fat red trout lay beside her.

Later, when they returned to the camp, the old woman scraped the remaining fat from the sealskin very carefully with her moon-shaped knife and soaked it in urine to remove all grease and to bleach the skin. Then she washed it many times in snow water and stretched it on a frame. The sharp night cold and the long sunlight glaring off the snow soon turned the skin sparkling white. Then the old woman cut the beautiful hide into careful patterns. She drew the finest bone needle from her little ivory case, and using the thinnest, strongest sinew, she soaked and shaped and sewed a pure white pair of knee-length boots. She did not give these boots to Kungo but hid them in her loonskin bag.

When the roof of the snowhouse collapsed on them from the heat of the spring sun, they all laughed with pleasure, for it was a sign that the geese would soon return and the fish would run once more in the open rivers. The old woman took many caribou skins and sewed them into a tent. Telikjuak cut the heavy sealskin thongs that held the long sled together, and using the runners to serve as tent poles, he covered them with the skins. This became their new summer home.

For two brief moons before the cold returned, millions of tiny insects swarmed in the clear, still air. The geese arrived in vast numbers to build their nests and to lay their eggs in the safety of the still marshlands where no man's foot had ever trod. Kungo and Telikjuak hunted and fished throughout the short summer.

But soon the tundra turned red with the coming of early autumn. Each morning new ice formed on every pond, and the winds carried within them the hidden whips of winter. The caribou were on the move again, trekking southward toward the Land of Little Sticks, their big antlers shining, their light autumn coats sleek and perfect for making warm clothing.

Early one morning when the air was sharp and the sky filled with heavy clouds, Kungo looked out of the tent and saw the old woman crouching alert and motionless on the far bank of the stream. Taking his bow and arrows, he hurried cautiously to the place where she waited for him. She nodded her head, and looking in that direction, he saw hundreds of caribou pouring along the bank of the river in single file, pawing the ground with their sharp hoofs and feeding. The young males threatened each other, raising their heads, shaking their great antlers, stepping stiffly sideways like graceful dancers.

Kungo strung his bow slowly so he would not frighten the animals and notched an arrow against the string. He aimed carefully at a plump bull caribou, its sides bulging from the rich summer feeding.

"Wait," whispered the old woman. "Look at that beautiful

58

one. Take that one," she urged.

He moved his bow until his line of sight seemed to reach out and touch the caribou with the light gray back and fine snow-white flanks. He released the arrow, and it silently flew straight to its mark. The animal reared up, ran out of the herd, and fell.

As he raised his bow again, the old woman called to him, "Quickly now, the one with the tan back and white belly."

Seeing it, he drove the arrow from his eye straight into its heart.

Three more she selected because of their whiteness, and three more he killed. Then the herd grew nervous, sensing danger, though they could not see or smell or hear it, and plunging through the shallow river, the caribou ran across the open plain. Swiftly they went, and so well did they blend with the autumn tundra that in a few moments they disappeared from view.

As they approached the place where the dead caribou lay, the old woman cried out with delight at the sight of such beautiful skins. Kungo helped her as they skillfully cut and stripped the soft hides from the animals.

"Telikjuak will bring the dogs to pack home the meat," she said, and rolling up the precious hides, she tied them and flung them onto her back. In her mind she was already planning the scraping, stretching, drying, pattern-cutting, and sewing of the new skins. She hummed a song as they returned to the tent. In each hand, Kungo carried a steaming red caribou liver as gifts for Telikjuak and the old man.

Later that autumn, after a blizzard, when the wind had packed great drifts in the river valley, they built a new snowhouse, the

first one of that winter. Taking down the tent poles, they lashed them together with crosspieces and remade their sled. Both the men and dogs felt the joy and excitement of the new winter with its sharp, invigorating cold. The open space of land and frozen sea became theirs once more to travel upon freely wherever they wished, and during the midwinter moon they decided to leave this inland hunting ground and return to the island.

They broke in the side of their snowhouse, fearing that evil spirits might lurk there and harm some other traveler. Then, like true nomads, they harnessed their dogs and drifted across the white expanse like leaves blown on the autumn wind.

When they reached the coast again, it was deadly cold, as the wind whipped in from the freezing sea, chilling a man until his bones trembled. In the second moon of winter, the long ice bridge formed and grew thick, and one early morning in the inky darkness they started to cross it. Before long, a storm blew in and the wind howled. The ice bridge heaved and cracked like a giant dog whip, but it held together, and by noon the next day they were safe in the shelter of the island's southern shore. Exhausted, they climbed up the steep passage, helping the old man, who could scarcely walk after their long, cold journey. When they entered the little stone house, the old woman lighted her lamp once more. It soon warmed the room and cast a soft glow among the bone rafters.

"It is good to travel far and to see each new day dawn over strange lands, for without moving we would not know the joy of returning home," she said, and the old man and Kungo nodded their heads in agreement. For the first time Kungo realized that

61

he now thought of this island, Tugjak, as his home, even though the painful dreams of his first home and lost family disturbed his sleep and caused his face sometimes to burn with anger.

On the following day, when Kungo first saw Lao and her family of dogs running together, he was afraid. Nine of them there were now, big and white and swift as young falcons. When he climbed the island's eastern slope, the wolf dogs raced straight at him. Then Kungo recognized Lao, who leaped and bounded around him, licking his hands. Two of her children snarled at him, but Lao warned them off with a growl. Although they were almost as large and strong as she, they obeyed her.

After the excitement of meeting again, Kungo looked at the half wolves, half dogs, all of which he had last seen as pups. They all had thick pure white coats, long heads, and the pale, frightening eyes of a wolf. Their legs were longer than their mother's, and the pads of their feet were wider, perfect for running on soft snow. Although no man had fed them during the year, they were strong and healthy, for they had learned to hunt for themselves. During the summer when game on the island was scarce, he knew they would have learned to stand belly-deep beyond the shore to snatch small fish from the water.

Kungo noticed one of them, lean and handsome, more wolf-like than the others, who lay like a white prince beside Lao. Its strange eyes were more piercing than the rest.

"Amahok," called Kungo, and the animal, answering to the name of wolf, leaped up and came quickly to the place where Kungo stood.

"You shall be the leader," said Kungo. But he did not touch the animal, for as it stood silently before him, he sensed the quick strength and wild fierceness that lay hidden in the white wolf dog.

All through the next spring, Kungo hunted seals and walrus that basked in the sunshine far out on the frozen sea. While hunting, he carefully trained the wolf dogs to work as a team, to obey his every command until they moved swiftly and quietly together during the hunt.

One day Telikjuak said to Kungo, "They are not wide-chested and strong like the best sled dogs that can pull great loads of meat, but they have long legs and can run like the wind. They do not fight much with each other, and they hunt for themselves. I have never seen such a team."

When Kungo fed them rich walrus meat, the wolf dogs grew

stronger and heavier, their chests widened, and their legs grew strong from pulling. All summer Kungo hunted food for the island camp. He practiced shooting from every angle with his bow. Telikjuak helped him make a long knife with a curved antler handle that he shaped and bound until it fitted his hand exactly. This he sharpened, stone blade against stone, until its edge was as sharp as a snow owl's claw.

One day they found a bleached driftwood log that had been washed up on the island shore by the tide. Telikjuak and Kungo split it by carefully driving sharp stone wedges along its center until it fell in two. Then they chipped these with short axes until the two pieces were shaped like long sled runners. These they left in the sun until they bleached bone-white. They made holes with a bow drill along the top of the wooden runners, and with seal thongs they lashed on other narrow slabs of driftwood for cross-pieces in order to hold the sled together.

The autumn came again, and Kungo knew that he was growing up. He was much stronger now, with great muscles in his arms and back from drawing the bow. He could heave his sled through the rough ice with ease. He often helped the powerful dwarf pull huge sides of walrus meat up from the sea to the place where they covered it with heavy stones to protect it from their dogs and wild animals. He felt glad to be alive and safe on their island home, and he thought of the old man and woman and the dwarf Telikjuak as his family. But deep inside him the restless hatred and the terrible desire to avenge his real family remained like a core of hard ice.

Kungo was determined to tell the old man of the anger that

64

burned within him, twisting his thoughts in the light of day and haunting his dreams at night.

One day Kungo saw the old man alone on the rust-colored moss some distance from the little house and thought that now was the time to speak with him. He noticed how bent with age the old man had become as he stood blinking blindly in the autumn sunlight. He seemed to be listening—listening to something far away.

"Telikjuak, Telikjuak," the old man called to the dwarf. "Bring me my bow. Bring Kigavik quickly."

Out of the cave came the dwarf, hobbling past Kungo as he unwrapped the soft caribou skin that protected Kigavik. One black arrow he carried, clenched between his teeth.

The old man took the great bow in his right hand like a staff, and thrusting it strongly downward, he snapped the bowstring into the upper notch. The dwarf handed him the arrow and moved away a few paces and crouched down. The old man dropped slowly, painfully, onto his knees, lifting his old face upward to the sky. His long white hair shifted about his shoulders in the light breeze, and his old eyes seemed weak and pale as mist.

Then Kungo heard the first sounds high and far away. It was the calling of the geese. Snow geese they were, sending their wild music down to the earth as they winged southwards from their summer nesting grounds. The very sound of them sent shivers up and down his spine.

Kungo could now see them flying in a high white wedge against the blue sky.

"Kungo! Kungo! Kungo!" called the geese, for the name the Eskimos had given them was the sound of their call and their name also. Kungo himself had been named for them.

The white geese were soon almost overhead, flying so high that they looked like drifting flakes of snow.

Kungo watched the old man kneeling motionless, lost in thought. Then Ittok slowly placed the dark arrow across Kigavik and carefully notched it in the sinew bowstring. With one powerful movement he raised Kigavik upward, drawing the great bow back as far as it would go. Smoothly he released the sinew, and with a mighty twang the arrow screamed into the sky.

Peering upward, Kungo shaded his eyes and waited. Then, high in the blue he saw the great white goose, the leader, at the very point of the wedge, stagger in its flight and start to fall. At first it turned over several times as its great white wings, out of control, were caught by the currents of air. Then it plunged straight downward, falling, falling. It struck the ground before them with a tremendous thud, its dead weight snapping the black arrow in half.

The dwarf crossed the opening and picked up the big bird. He brought it to the old man, who remained kneeling on the ground, holding the great bow, Kigavik, curved in his hands like the swift dark wings of a falcon.

"These are feathers for a white archer. It is right that you should have them. But you must never kill this bird nor eat its flesh, for you bear its name. You came to us from the wild geese, and when you die, your spirit will fly free and live with the snow geese once more. They are a part of you."

Kungo took the wild goose gently in his hands. It was soft and warm and heavy, and the beautiful head on the slender neck curved back until it almost touched the ground. The powerful wing feathers lay open in death, white as wave tops, curved one against the other like wind-carved drifts of snow.

Kungo wished to speak with the old man, but the right time never seemed to come. Ittok was now almost completely blind, and much of the time he sat nodding back and forth lost in thought. It was as though his body remained with them and his mind went away, traveling in the distant lands of his youth.

One night when the old man was asleep, Kungo quietly told the old woman of his troubled thoughts and that he must go and search the inland for the Indians who had destroyed his family. The memory of that terrible night burned within him like fire and would not let him rest.

The old woman stopped sewing and nodded sadly.

"Yes," she said, looking at her sleeping husband. "He told me four years ago that you would remain until the ice bridge formed this winter and that you would then go forth, driven by your desire to avenge your family. That time has now come, but I must say to you that hatred and revenge follow each other like two strong men piling heavy stones one upon the other until the stones fall, killing both men and perhaps many others."

Kungo heard her words but did not try to understand their meaning, so crowded was his mind with the wild spirit of vengeance. Over and over again he planned the journey in his mind, for he knew that he must go. He must be ready when the ice bridge formed during the midwinter moon.

Silently the dwarf helped him make new arrows, long and straight, with points as sharply ground as a weasel's tooth. To these arrows they carefully bound the feathers freshly plucked from the wings of the wild snow goose. Sadly the old woman made eight strong white sealskin harnesses for the team.

Kungo ran the white wolf dogs every day and heaved the long sled until he, the driver, and his team grew wise and strong as they worked together. When he called to the leader, Amahok, to stop or go, lead right or left, the wolf dog obeyed instantly and the team followed willingly.

One biting cold morning at the end of the first winter moon, Kungo climbed the high stone cliff that surrounded their little house. From Tugjak's highest peak he looked toward the distant mainland and saw that the long ice bridge had formed. He hurried down and told the old couple that if the weather remained good, he would leave the following day.

When he awoke the next morning, a new fur parka with a full hood and new knee-length fur pants lay beside him on the bed. They were cut and finely sewn from the flanks of the caribou he had hunted on the inland plain. He had never seen anything so beautiful. He pulled these over his light inner parka and pants and found that they fitted perfectly. The outer parka and pants were white as snow, and the wolf-trimmed hood rested warmly around his neck. He then put on two pairs of thick, warm fur stockings, knee high, and over these he drew the snug-fitting white sealskin boots.

The old woman, who had made the pure white clothing for him, was still sitting by her lamp. She smiled at him in a sad way and handed him the last three items, a tight hat made of white weasel skins, a pair of white fur mitts with leather palms, and a small white bag of grease and ashes.

There were no words that Kungo could find to say to the old woman, and as he thought of all her songs and the joys they had shared during their long walks over the summer tundra, he felt a great sadness rise up in him. Picking up his white bag, he turned and hurried out of the house, for he could not bring himself to look at her.

The old man stood beside the entrance. The dog Lao was close beside him. His old eyes seemed not to see Kungo, but with fumbling hands he reached down and grasped the great bow, Kigavik. He held it out before him.

"With this bow I give you all my strength and power, my gift to see and understand. Take it. Use it wisely. Take it quickly," he said as the tears ran out of his blind eyes.

Kungo looked at the old man and at Kigavik quivering like the wings of a dark falcon in the old man's hands. He laid his own white bow at the old man's feet and took the big bow gently. He tried to but could not speak. Slowly he turned and walked away down the long snow-filled path that led to the sea ice.

Telikjuak had harnessed the team of white wolf dogs down below the cliffs on the frozen sea. The dwarf did not look at Kungo as he tightened the leather lashings on the sled. Spread over the sled was the dwarf's sleeping skin made from the great white bear he had killed.

"You need that bearskin for sleeping in the cave," said Kungo, starting to take the huge skin off the sled.

"Leave it on," the dwarf commanded in a harsh, rough voice that Kungo had not heard before. "It is yours, white archer. Now, go with strength. Fly with Kigavik," he said, and gave a sharp warning command to the wolf dogs, who howled and strained in their harnesses, eager to start the journey.

"Ush! Ush!" Kungo called to the lead dog, and as the sled headed forward, he jumped onto it.

When the team had settled into a steady running pace across the snow-covered ice, Kungo turned to look back. He saw the little dwarf figure standing alone before the jagged rocks of the island, peering after the team with his sharp eyes. But Kungo knew that the whiteness of his clothing and the white sled and team had caused him to disappear like magic into the great whiteness of the ice bridge.

The wolf team traveled so fast that Kungo dared not run beside the sled to keep warm for fear he might fall behind. He grew cold and would have frozen on the wind-whipped sled had it not been for his new and perfect-fitting clothing. The deep fur-trimmed hood protected his face from the stinging cold, and almost before he knew it, the team had carried him safely across the ice bridge. They reached the coast of the mainland before the winter moon had risen.

Kungo halted the team with one sharp command and, walking forward, unharnessed the wolf dogs, calling each one by its name. From a rough skin bag on the sled, he shook out rich chunks of frozen seal meat that the hungry team devoured in an instant. Sitting quietly on the sled in the still cold, he watched the evening star rise above the coastal hills, while with his knife he shaved and ate thin delicious pieces of the frozen seal meat, the same food he had given to the team.

Kungo then quickly built a small igloo, using his long ivory-bladed snow knife to cut and shape the blocks of wind-packed snow. He cut the blocks in a circle from below his feet and built the walls of the house around himself. Crawling out of the entrance after the blocks were in place, he filled the cracks with snow. Then he gently pushed Kigavik and the skin of the great white bear into the igloo and crawled inside before fitting the snow-block door in place. He carefully pulled off his white outer parka and pants and rolled himself in his new sleeping skin that Telikjuak had given him.

Now he was truly alone, with a terrible task to perform. Lying there in the small igloo, he thought again of the dark night of the Indians and of his parents, lost to him forever, of his sister, Shulu, stolen from his sight. Terrible anger ran within him, and he lay shaking in the warm bearskin as though he were chilled to the bone. When the shaking passed, he drifted off to sleep and dreamed of Indians, lean, gaunt men with faces painted in wild designs.

The next morning he arose long before the light came into the eastern sky. He cut the igloo open with his knife and stepped out. In an instant the team was up, and he harnessed each dog. He placed Kigavik carefully in its long protective quiver beside the separate pouch that held the arrows. He tucked it carefully between the soft folds of the white bearskin. This, along with the meat bag, he lashed to the long sled.

With a call to Amahok, the lead dog, he set the dogs in

motion. The whole team leaped forward and rushed southward, following the coast. He called commands to Amahok, who led the team with a long, loping stride.

Two snowhouses he built and three days they traveled on the sea ice until they came to the barrier ice heaved up at the mouth of a great frozen river. Turning, they followed inland the broad path of snow-covered ice. Kungo searched the snowy banks on either side, for it reminded him of his homeland as a child. But he could see no igloos, no sign of life in this lonely place, and the team carried him swiftly forward, following the river as it curved between the coastal hills.

The second night he stopped, fed the team, built his snowhouse, and, sitting on the sled, ate his only meal of the day. Kungo watched the moon rise up like a giant's eye and cast its long light in a narrow shining path across the hills. He heard the river ice crack and groan in the still cold as though some monster lay hidden and strained to be released. Although Kungo had never seen the little people, he knew that it was at a time like this a man could hear the river spirits laughing and the answering whistle of the shore spirits. He watched along the river carefully, for it had always been said that the little people of the spirit world loved to crawl out of a crack and lie upon their backs on the ice, kicking up their legs and chuckling in the very path of the moonlight. He thought perhaps he heard a small laughing sound, but in the pale light he saw nothing.

Then all was silent. The wolf dogs lay quietly around the snowhouse, and Kungo curled up in the warmth of his sleeping skin and slept until morning.

The third and fourth days' journey carried him far across the inland plain, and on the fifth day a great blizzard swept over the land. At first the air grew warm and huge flakes of snow whirled down, the wind whipped itself into a fury, and Kungo could not see the dogs before him.

He stopped and built an igloo, though the wind was so violent that it tore some of the snow blocks from his hands. He fed the dogs the last scraps of seal meat and crawled into his igloo, where he slept and dreamed and waked and thought and slept again. For five days the winds thundered against his little house and tried to tear it from the land, but he had built it well and it stood firmly until the wind went moaning off across the plain, leaving only a vast white silence.

When at last Kungo cut away the snow door and stepped outside, it was like a white magic place. The giants hidden in the wind had carved the snow into wild shapes, piling great drifts against the riverbanks. They had swept the lake ice clear of snow. Everything had changed, and the leaden-colored storm clouds hid the sun and stars and would not tell him east from west.

Kungo bent down and with his bare hands felt beneath the snow, for under this new snow he knew that the old drifts ran north and south. When he moved his hands along the old hard ridges, he learned the direction that he must travel. Harnessing the team, he set out more slowly now. The dogs, like himself, were hungry from the five days' fasting.

They camped that evening on the edge of a low ridge that ran south as far as he could see. This ridge was what Kungo

had been looking for. From its height he could see any movement of men or animals crossing the plain.

On the following day they journeyed straight south along the ridge. Kungo searched east and west but saw nothing until almost evening when, with a short command, he stopped the team. Far out beyond his right hand on the flat plain, he was aware of some movement. He watched and waited carefully. Then in the distance he made out a long line of caribou, looking like spots of silver on the horizon, slowly moving north. Kungo was very hungry, the wolf team could not continue much longer without food, and he knew he might not see game again in this desolate country. But the flame of anger in him said, "Go on. *Go forward now.*"

He called a command to Amahok, and the team pulled on until the waning moon rose again. Then Kungo built another snowhouse and slept fitfully, for he was now weak with hunger.

When he stepped from his igloo in the morning, he saw a welcome sight. The wolf dogs lay before the entrance, their white coats stained with blood, and he knew in an instant that they had run silently as a free hunting pack in the night and had pulled down a caribou, fed themselves, and returned to him. There was a look of triumph in the green eyes of Amahok and the others as they lay with full bellies licking their white coats clean.

For two days they traveled south, seeing nothing in the land save one snowy owl searching like themselves across the white expanse.

Late the following afternoon Kungo saw in the distance the

Land of Little Sticks. He had never seen it before. The small trees stood like gray ghosts silently listening on the plain. Beyond these first dwarfed trees, he could see there were larger ones and many more of them.

He camped early because he did not wish to sleep among the little sticks and because he feared that the dogs would tangle their long lines in the trees. Before he entered his new snow-house, he looked around him in the twilight and listened carefully, and he knew fear inside himself. He was starving. He cut a piece of leather dog line and chewed it, hoping this would give him strength.

That night strange dreams whirled through his mind. When one of the wolf dogs gave a long, sad howl at the moon, he leaped up almost before he was awake and found himself crouched and ready, facing the entrance, his knife clutched in his hand.

He was out of the little house the next morning and had the wolf dogs harnessed before the moon grew pale. Before he had gone far, he saw the three stone men. These images must be the ones mentioned by the lean man from the River of Two Tongues. This surely was the place. Then he saw the sight that he had dreamed about for four long years, the frozen river that led into the Land of Little Sticks, and far away, almost on the southern horizon, thin columns of smoke rising in the still morning air. There were not ten fires, as the three men had seen long ago, but more than twenty.

He sat down on the sled, starving and alone. He remembered the terrible vision of his childhood, of the strong, lean men with

78

bows and knives and clubs, of the big man lying with the arrows in his back.

But Kungo started off again, driving the team cautiously toward the camp, following the river between the little sticks, and peering fearfully into every shadow. It was growing milder now, and the air was soft.

He halted the wolf dogs, and they lay down in the snow. He drew Kigavik with its arrow quiver from beneath the lashings and turned the sled over to act as an anchor to hold the team. Then, slinging the bow and quiver across his back and checking that his long knife was safe in his boot, he started carefully forward. The soft snow, once he had left the banks of the river, was almost knee-deep.

He walked through the little sticks, guided by the thin columns of smoke rising before him, until he came to the top of a small hill. There spread before him was the Indian camp where he guessed at least twenty families must live. Never, in his whole life, had he seen a place with so many people crowded together.

The shape of their tents was utterly strange to him. They were cones built of many long sticks with skins stretched tightly around them. White acid-smelling smoke rose from the opening at the top of every tent. Men he saw, and women and children, and many thin dogs. The men looked tall and dangerous, and there were many of them. He thought of himself, so young and yet planning to go alone against a huge camp of Indian warriors. Again he felt the terrible pangs of hunger and fear, but deep inside himself he knew that he must act—and quickly before his strength failed him.

When it was dark, he slowly returned through the deep, heavy snow to the river and his team. He could not build an igloo, for the snow was too soft among the trees. Instead he rolled himself in the white bearskin and lay among his wolf dogs, hoping they would give him protection.

When he awoke, the land was covered with a light silver fog and big snowflakes drifted lazily down through the small trees. He rose and staggered off, dizzy from hunger as he once more left the dogs and made his way toward the dreaded Indian camp. He remembered his father telling him that a starving man could live without food for a whole moon as long as he had snow to eat or water.

A sound behind made him whirl quickly and snatch at his knife before he saw that it was Amahok who had worked free of the harness. The white lead dog stared at him with wise green eyes, and when Kungo moved forward again, the animal followed silently in his footsteps.

Kungo chose a different route this time because he wanted to go to a small frozen lake that he had seen near the Indian camp. He stumbled occasionally in the strange foggy light that made all shadows disappear and distances difficult to judge.

Now Kungo stood beside the snow-covered lake and looked across at the Indian fires. He drew the white weasel cap from his parka hood and placed it on his head so that it covered his black hair. He pulled the small leather pouch from inside his parka and rubbed the mixture of white grease and ashes on his face and hands. Amahok remained beside Kungo, sniffing the strong smoky scent of the camp.

For a long time Kungo stood stock-still out on the lake, looking up through the mists, searching for courage, while fearful visions of Indians raced through his mind. Suddenly he shouted in a terrible voice, "*Dog people. Women killers. Kayak rippers. Igloo breakers. Come to me. Come to me now in the dear morning.*"

He then howled like a wolf, and Amahok joined him in a frightening chorus. Next he cried out like a loon laughing across a lonely lake. And last he roared like a bear fighting against many dogs.

There was a moment of silence in the Indian camp, followed by excited voices in a strange language that Kungo could not understand. Among the trees he could see men running, bent forward like hunters fitting arrows into their bows as they rushed toward him. He screamed once more, like an angry falcon, and they all stopped and raised their bows.

Slowly he reached behind him and drew Kigavik from his back. With his right hand he selected six white arrows from the quiver and stood them in the snow before him. A flight of Indian arrows struck around him. Some were very close.

He notched a seventh arrow in the bowstring and lowered his head in thought. Then he raised Kigavik and aimed the sharp point straight into the heart of the nearest crouching warrior. But at that moment something strange happened to him.

A whirlwind of doubts rushed into his mind. If he harmed these people now, would they not wait and seek revenge again among his people? Would they not come yet again into the Eskimo land, raiding and killing, carrying the old hatred forward

82

from father to son to grandson? Was he not helping to pile hatred upon hatred like stones that might fall and kill everyone? Was he indeed any better in his quest for revenge than a mad dog that seeks only to bite and kill? Had the three starving men of his own kind not caused all this trouble long ago by raiding the Indian camp and stealing meat?

A vision of the old woman's face seemed to drift before his eyes. Kungo remembered all her gentleness and the wise things she had said to him. He moved the point of his arrow away from the Indian's heart. But his anger was not entirely spent. His eyes narrowed, and he clenched his teeth as he sent the arrow whistling into the heavy collar of the warrior's skin coat. It pierced through the fur collar and cut into his strange hat, pinning them together. The arrow then pressed so tightly across the Indian's throat that he screamed in terror.

Kungo sent arrow after arrow whistling in among the warriors, ripping their clothing, terrifying them, but never killing them. The Indians took aim but held back their second flight of arrows, for they could not see Kungo disguised and hidden in his whiteness. He moved like a silver shadow disappearing in the mists and snow, and they cried out in fear.

They saw clearly the great bow Kigavik, curved like a black falcon's wings, that rose and fell menacingly. Its bowstring sang. Its arrows flew against them, guided by the wild-goose feathers. The Indians were sure this was some winter spirit with a magic bow.

When Kungo's arrows were almost spent, he heard a soft woman's voice among the rough strange shouting of the Indians.

It called to him. It called to him in Eskimo. It called his name.

"Kungo. Kungo. Brother of mine, I know your voice. I beg you, put down your bow. I am Shulu, your sister."

The Indians watched in terror. They did not know whether to stand or run as the Eskimo girl, Shulu, walked out alone across the snowy lake to the place where the black bow hung poised in the air.

When Shulu stood before her brother, she rubbed her hand over her eyes, for she could scarcely see him.

"Brother of mine," she said, "are you a ghost? Or have you come to me after all these years when I have thought you dead."

She reached out timidly and put her hand against his cheek to feel if he were real. Then she took his hand gently and began to lead him across the lake.

The warriors stood back as she led Kungo through them into the very center of the Indian camp. A hundred dark eyes stared out at them from the tents and snowy cover of the trees, watching the falcon bow, the great white wolf dog, and this faint ghostlike shadow of a man.

Amahok stalked close beside Kungo, his muscles tensed, ready to spring. A low growl rumbled steadily in his throat, and his green wolf eyes stared suspiciously around him, for he did not trust this place or these strange people.

Kungo, like the wolf dog, was tense and uneasy. None of this was right. None of it was as he had planned it all these years. He had not taken revenge upon these people because of the vision of the old woman, and now helpless and outnumbered among these warriors, he felt that they would surely kill him.

84

He eyed his sister walking beside him; her clothing was completely strange to him. It was made of caribou skin with all the hair scraped away, and it had no hood. It hung evenly to her knees, where it ended in a long, dangling fringe. Her costume was painted with strange red and black border designs of a kind he had never seen. Below the skirt long caribou skin leggings, fringed on the side, hung down to her moccasined feet. On her head she wore a round decorated cap, and her long hair was braided in an unfamiliar way. Strings of bright beads hung around her neck.

Kungo tightened his grip on the long knife that was now concealed in the sleeve of his parka when a dark shadowy figure moved quickly from the shelter of the trees. It was an Indian who went and waited near the entrance of the tent that stood in their path. He was tall and lean, scarcely older than Kungo, dressed in a costume not unlike Shulu's. Over his knee-length coat he wore a wide beaded belt and across his shoulder a wonderfully decorated game bag. His hat was shaped and pointed in a strange and handsome fashion. He stood still, full of dignity, like a hawk, alert and ready to strike. Kungo noticed that he had removed the mitten from his right hand, and it hung tense and ready beside his long iron knife. His face was dark and handsome, but it seemed carved of stone and told Kungo nothing.

Shulu spoke to the young man rapidly in a strange high-singing sound.

She then turned to Kungo and said, "This is Natawa. He knows now that you are my brother." Then she went quickly into the tent.

86

The tall young Indian held back the skin flap that served as a cover for the entrance. Kungo stepped over a long log and found himself inside the dark interior. Amahok lay down on guard outside.

Once inside, Kungo waited until his eyes became accustomed to the dark. The tent was round inside, with the caribou-skin walls sloping upward to the blackened smoke hole in the center of the roof. Many caribou skins and some brightly colored blankets were piled against the sides of the tent for sleeping. A round flat drum made of stretched caribou skin hung by a long leather thong from the tent poles. In the very center, within a small circle of stones, Kungo could see some glowing embers and the long log he had crossed at the entrance that was the main fuel for the fire. The log was never cut but merely pushed further and further into the flames. A large iron pot simmered over the fire.

Shulu led her brother to a special place by the fire and arranged the thickest skins for him to sit upon. The lean young Indian stepped inside the tent and squatted down across the fire from Kungo. Much of his face was caught by the firelight, but his eyes were lost in shadow, and Kungo could not read his face or guess what he was thinking. Kungo saw the place where his arrow had torn open the skin of the Indian's garment at the throat.

"This man, Natawa, is my husband," said Shulu. "We have been married together since the first moon of summer."

Kungo felt the cords of his neck thicken, for he could scarcely believe the words he heard.

Seeing the look on her brother's face, Shulu added quickly, "You must be hungry, brother of mine," and bent forward to stir the rich yellow broth that covered soft chunks of caribou meat.

Kungo refused the meat and remained silent, watching the Indian carefully, ready for any sudden movement. He knew by the sound of Amahok's low growl that the tent must now be surrounded by bowmen.

"For all these years," said Shulu, "I have feared that you and all my relatives were dead. When they first brought me here, I was always afraid. The children laughed at me and threw stones at me, and I was only used to carry water and skin out birds. But later I was adopted and had a mother and father. I learned to speak the language of these people, and all the children became my friends, and my new mother and father were always kind to me and taught me many things. Now I speak slowly and badly to you in our own tongue, brother of mine, because I have almost forgotten my own language.

"Sometimes in spring my soul cries out as I look across the barrens and remember how it used to be. I think again of times long ago when you and I made the long trek inland with our family. I remember the snow geese that laid their eggs on the soft tundra and the fat red and silver trout that drifted under the holes in the melting lake ice. I will never forget the night skies of the far north in summer when the sun walked on the hilltops and it never grew dark.

"But that is long passed now, like a dream. I am here among the little sticks with these people, and I think of them as my people. I wish that you could know Natawa as I know him and that he could know you as I know you. You and Natawa might have killed each other out there on the ice of the lake, and even now across the fire I see you each watching the knife hand of the other. I am only a foolish girl, but now I understand how wrong that is. I have love for both of you, and I have seen each of you dancing, singing, laughing, crying, and I know that, though you speak strange languages, you are truly brothers."

Then turning her gaze toward Natawa, Shulu said many words that Kungo could not understand. Looking at her, Natawa's face softened, and he knelt forward and drew his iron knife from his belt. He drove it into the big pot and caught a great chunk of meat on its point. Turning the handle toward Kungo, he offered him the knife and then lay back on the pile of soft skins.

Kungo shook the long knife from his sleeve and pushed it aside. Then he placed the big bow, Kigavik, behind him. His hunger returned to him in a rush, and as he smelled the rich meat, he remembered that he was starving. Not wishing to show his hunger, he ate slowly, savoring every bite until he was full.

Natawa stepped outside and spoke to the people who had waited there, and after he had spoken, the bowmen returned to their tents and Amahok ceased to growl.

Almost all that night, Kungo told them of his life after he had last seen his sister, and Shulu interpreted this to her husband.

When Kungo had finished speaking, Natawa then told him of the time he had first seen Shulu when they were young, of their marriage and of the long adventure they had shared that autumn. They had paddled south in a canoe on a wide river with many white rapids whose banks were covered with tall trees. Natawa's white teeth flashed as he smiled and spoke of a country that seemed filled with wild animals of a kind that Kungo had never

90

seen. He spoke of black bears, of big red-headed birds that hammered the high branches like drummers, and great furry animals that climbed in the trees. He said these creatures had spotted coats, yellow eyes, and the long sharp claws of an eagle.

Toward morning they lay down on the soft furs, covered themselves with colored blankets, and slept together. When they awoke, Kungo gave a start, for he could not remember at first where he was.

Shulu rose first and pushed the long log further into the embers of the fire so that it started to blaze briskly, and she placed the meat pot closer to the flames.

Natawa spoke to her for a long time, and when he was finished, she turned and said to Kungo, "He asks you to stay with us, to stay among his people. He asks you to join him in forgiving old wrongs, to hunt together with him, to fish with us when we travel to the high falls on the Singing River when it is springtime again, and to live together like brothers. Oh, will you, Kungo? Will you do as he asks?"

"Tell him that I understand the things that you have said for him, that I would like to hunt with him and learn to speak with him, and that I am sorry about the arrow that came so close to his throat. I am horrified by the thought that yesterday I had it in my mind to kill him.

"I must return to the island, for the old people have become my family and I must help them. When I have seen that they are well and have food enough, I shall return to meet you at the high falls in the spring."

Together they left the tent and walked out through the Indian camp. Big flakes of soft snow drifted down through the dark trees, catching on and clinging to the branches and to the sides of the smoke-stained tents. Before each of these dwellings hung rich beaver and otter pelts stretched on sapling frames to dry. Shulu had told Kungo the night before that the Indians prized these furs as trimming for their clothing. It was also their custom, she had said, to trade fur with strangers further south for iron knives, pots, beads, and blankets.

As Kungo walked, small Indian children, as motionless as frightened rabbits, peered out at him from the tents. They watched carefully, for he was almost invisible in his white fur clothing against the snowy background. Behind Kungo strode the yellow-eyed wolf dog.

When they came to a grove of trees, Natawa pulled delicately laced snowshoes from his back, slipped his moccasined feet into their bindings, and stepped off the trodden path. He traveled easily, with a swinging gait, over the top of the soft new snow until he arrived at the place where heavy haunches of caribou hung from the trees. Reaching up, he pulled four of these down and loaded them onto a toboggan that stood nearby. Throwing the line over his shoulders, he hauled the toboggan to the path, and with Shulu's help he followed Kungo across the lake and through the little sticks until they came to the place where Kungo's team waited patiently.

After the white wolf dogs were fed, Kungo gave a short command, and they leaped into position, ready to go, waiting for the second command.

Kungo looked into his sister's face and then at Natawa. The

Indian stared back at him, his dark eyes narrowed as if in pain. He said one short sentence to Shulu and was silent.

Shulu said, "He asks me if I wish to go with you. He says that he will hide his eyes if I wish to go with you."

One word she replied to Natawa.

Then to Kungo she said, "I will always stay with him. But come as he asks in spring and fish with us at the high falls between the two lands."

Kungo turned and faced Natawa, and in the ancient way of his people, he dropped his mitts on the snow and pushed back the sleeves of his parka to the elbow, showing that he concealed no weapons against the man before him. Natawa, understanding this gesture, drew back his own sleeves and stepped forward. Their fingers touched briefly, and without any spoken words they understood each other.

Kungo called out to the dogs. They lunged forward and rushed out of the Land of Little Sticks toward the open wind-swept tundra. He looked back once and saw his sister, Shulu, standing silently beside her husband. A warm feeling spread through his body as he thought of her, alive and happy. All his anger was gone from him, gone, he hoped, forever.

Then the sharp sting of cold struck him, and he laughed aloud with pleasure. He was returning to his own land. He would travel to the island of Tugjak and talk with the old man again. Ittok was a great teacher and had taught him many things about archery and about life. The old woman had tempered his feelings for revenge and had helped him to understand himself. They were his people.

Kungo shouted with joy. Soon he would see the dwarf once more and hear the songs of the old woman. Shulu was safe. His wolf dogs ran fast. The great falcon bow, Kigavik, was lashed safely to his sled. But, best of all, when the spring sun came and released the river at the high falls, he knew he would see his sister and Natawa.

A great happiness rose up in him, and suddenly the words of a song rushed into him from the sky, and knowing them, feeling them inside himself, he sang them boldly into the very teeth of the north wind. His ears, once hearing the words, would remember them forever:

> "Ayii, Ayii, Ayii, Ayii,
> I walked on the ice of the sea
> And wondering I heard
> The song of the sea,
> The great sighing of new-formed ice.
> Go then, go, strength of soul,
> Bring health to the place of feasting.
> Ayii, Ayii."